Puberty
Children's Stories

Johny Takkedasila

Ukiyoto Publishing

All global publishing rights are held by

Ukiyoto Publishing

Published in 2024

Content Copyright © Johny Takkedasila

ISBN 9789360496883

All rights reserved.
No part of this publication may be reproduced, transmitted, or stored in a retrieval system, in any form by any means, electronic, mechanical, photocopying, recording or otherwise, without the prior permission of the publisher.

The moral rights of the author have been asserted.

This book is sold subject to the condition that it shall not by way of trade or otherwise, be lent, resold, hired out or otherwise circulated, without the publisher's prior consent, in any form of binding or cover other than that in which it is published.

www.ukiyoto.com

With love and responsibility to all children in the world.

Contents

Puberty	1
Breast Bud	4
The Forest	7
Voice	10
Periods	13
Misconception	16
A Natural Discomfort	19
Short	22
Identity	25
Dissatisfaction	29
Fickle	33
Digital Identity	37
Privacy	41
Testicles	44
Stress	47
About the Author	*54*

Puberty

Ramu is studying in the seventh standard. He is very active in both studies and games, and he is liked by everyone at school and home due to his intelligence and kindness.

He is currently studying diligently as the 7th class exams are approaching, and this time, his determination to secure the first rank is strong.

@@@

Ramu studied for a while and then slept next to his mother. In the middle of the night, he woke up feeling something wet. His whole body trembled, and he rushed into the bathroom.

The underwear he was wearing felt sticky, and upon untying it, some white liquid appeared. Seeing that, Ramu's eyes rolled. He felt confused and scared.

Until then, nothing like that had happened. Ramu couldn't understand why it was so white from the urethra, and this confusion left him feeling troubled. He washed himself with water and went back to sleep next to his mother.

From that day onward, Ramu felt fear, irritation, and confusion. He struggled to read properly, always getting distracted despite putting books in front of him.

Even though Ramu lives in a joint family, still he did not know whom to tell his problem.

@@@

Ramu's grandmother noticed that at an age when he should be playing, singing, and eating his favorite things, he was silent, distracted, scared, and fearful.

One day, she called Ramu and said, 'What happened? You have been distracted for a few days. Did anything happen at school?' she asked.

'No,' he said, shaking his head.

Grandmother got suspicious when Ramu, who used to talk loudly, was silently shaking his head.

'Did your father say anything?' she tried to ask again.

He staggered away from his grandmother and went outside.

Grandmother inquired with Ramu's parents. No one said anything at home. So, she again thought that something might have happened at school only. She wanted to ask about the matter with Ramu.

@@@

Everyone went to bed after eating as usual. However, Ramu slept a little away from his mother, and Grandma noticed that. Later, upon noticing Ramu going to the bathroom in the middle of the night and coming back to bed scared, grandmother came to an idea about Ramu's problem.

After Ramu came home from school, she took him with her to the farm.

'Are you studying well? Is there any problem at school?' She slowly tried to find the matter.

'He shook his head nervously, saying that there was no problem.'

'Isn't your health good!?'

Ramu did not speak; after a while, he wept bitterly.

She hugged Ramu and asked, "What happened, my boy? You're usually so active. I realized something was wrong when you got quiet and seemed afraid." She looked at him with love, encouraging him to share what happened.

'I won't live long,' he cried, 'I'm sick.'

'Such words should not be spoken,' Grandmother wiped away Ramu's tears and consoled him, encouraging him to tell her what happened.

'Ramu tells what happened to him.'

'Are you afraid of this?' She started telling him to listen carefully.

"The white matter that comes out of the urethra at this age is called 'semen.' It happens to all men. If you wait for a few more days, your school will tell you about it in detail. If you get 'sperm,' it means you are getting older. It is a happy thing but not a sad thing."

"Some people do that in their sleep. Others do not. After reaching a certain age, it is natural for our body to undergo changes. Without thinking too much about it, just go to the bathroom and clean up when that happens. Not only that, your body will undergo many changes in the coming days. Ask me if you have any doubts without fearing it," she said and hugged him lovingly.

After listening to his grandmother's words, Ramu felt relieved. He was now prepared for the changes in his body. He understood that it was not a disease but a common thing that happened to him and everyone his age. He thought that he should ask his grandmother whenever he had any questions, misunderstandings, or problems.

Grandmother told Ramu's father to explain such things clearly to Ramu.

***

Note: It is the responsibility of parents to educate children about such things at the right time and right age.

Breast Bud

Bittu and Ricky are brothers. Ricky is in the eighth standard, while Bittu is in the sixth standard. Their father, Surya works in a municipal office, and their mother is a home-maker. Surya originally belongs to Proddatur in Kadapa district, but now he lives in Tirupati due to work reasons.

On Sundays, when Bittu and Ricky were at home, they were often found quarreling. The main source of their quarrel was the mobile phone.

Bittu enjoys playing games on the mobile, while Ricky prefers watching reels on Instagram.

Ricky's father bought a mobile for the children so that they could learn technology and use it for project work.

However, since the arrival of the mobile in the house, the quarrels between the children have increased.

@@@

'You've been looking at Instagram for an hour! I want to play games,' Bittu went over to Ricky, demanding the phone. Both of them pushed and pulled each other. Bittu clenched his fist and punched Ricky hard in the chest.

Ricky, who had been experiencing pain in his nipples on both sides of the chest for a few days, shouted loudly.

Ricky's father, Surya, who was working in his room, ran to the children. Bittu ran to his mother. Surya lifted Ricky, who had fallen down, and made him sit up.

'What happened? Why did you cry? Did he hit you hard?' Surya was afraid.

Ricky's mother had already arrived there. Seeing Ricky holding his hand over his heart and crying, she looked at her husband, asking him to take Ricky to the hospital.

'Why do we need to go to the hospital for something so small?' He said and asked Ricky to take off his shirt to check for any injuries.

Ricky refused to take off his shirt. Surya took Ricky to the room and asked him to show. When Ricky took off his shirt, both sides of his chest were red and swollen near the nipples.

Surya understood the matter. 'Does it hurt?' he asked lovingly. Ricky hugged his father, saying, 'Dad, I have been in pain for two days.'

'If the pain is too much, you should have said so, dear!' He said.

He told his wife and took Ricky to the hospital.

@@@

The doctor examined Ricky, and said that it is normal to have pain near the nipples at this age. Some people may experience more pain, but there is no need to take special medicines for this.

Understanding Ricky's shock, confusion, and bewilderment. He sent Surya out, saying that Ricky might be uncomfortable if his father was present.

'Look, Ricky! I understand that you are confused. Do you want to ask anything?' he asked calmly.

'Why do I have this pain? Is this a disease? When I asked my friend, he joked, "Why did you get the pain that girls should get?"'

Understanding Ricky's concern, the doctor explained about breast buds.

"We should not feel bad when someone says something without knowing or understanding. It is not a disease as you think. It is not only girls who experience this, but boys as well."

"This pain can occur any time after the age of ten. The main reason for that is the growth of the body. This pain is because of the breast bud. A small bump appears on the inside of the nipples. It will be painful, but it will subside within a few days or months."

"As you get older, there are changes in hormones, and because of that, the nipples grow. You must have already noticed many changes in your body. Remember that all this is to make your body strong and healthy."

"If you have any doubts, you should ask your father. There should be no shame or discomfort with your father. If the pain is too much, come with your father."

'What did the doctor say?' Surya asked Ricky, who happily came out of the room.

Ricky boldly told his father what the doctor had said without shame, fear.

***

Note: Parents of children entering puberty should recognize the need to be friends and discuss such matters.

The Forest

Arun is the only son of Krishna Mohan and Parvati. Arun is studying in the ninth standard at Venkatappa Memorial High School. He likes kabaddi and shuttle very much, and also does not neglect his studies.

There are mandal-level kabaddi competitions in Pulivendula within a few months. The principal instructed the P.E.T. Peter that Arun's team should win at any cost. That's why Peter is training Arun's team in the evening, especially in kabaddi.

Peter likes Arun a lot because he plays sports well. Arun is confident that the team will make it to the Mandal level this time anyway.

There is a ground one kilometer from the school, where all the children go in the evening to play sports like cricket, shuttle, and kabaddi.

As usual, Peter took Arun and the team to the ground. Both teams played kabaddi smartly and enthusiastically. Arun was playing the game well, but in the middle, he put his hands between his thighs and scratched himself awkwardly. His friends noticed it and laughed. Unable to focus on his game, Arun's team lost.

Peter, puzzled by Arun's behavior, asked, "What happened? Why are you not focused on the game? I thought we would win. Any problem?"

"Nothing, sir. I assure you that our team will win tomorrow for sure."

The next day, during the school break, Arun went to urinate along with his friends. While Arun was urinating, Chakri looked at

Arun and joked saying forest. Arun, understanding the joke, got angry and went to beat him, but the friends intervened.

Later, in the classroom, Chakri shouted loudly saying 'Forest, Forest.'

Arun felt embarrassed and decided not to go to school. Krishna Mohan, Arun's father, scolded him for not attending school.

Arun went to school but remained silent and did not talk to anyone. Kabaddi was not played properly in the evening either.

Taking aside, Peter asked Arun gently, "What happened? Why are you sad? You are not focused on playing Kabaddi either."

No words came from Arun and He lowered his head in silence.

Two or three times while Peter was talking, Arun scratched the sensitive area between his thighs.

"Look, Arun, I am your father's age, so you can share anything with me. I can help you if I know what your problem is. Don't feel sad inside without saying anything." Peter lovingly put his hand on Arun's shoulder and asked softly.

"Chakri is making fun of me, sir. I seem to have lost my dignity in front of everyone due to hair in my underarms and near the sensitive area, it's causing itching."

Peter understood and explained, "It is normal to get pubic hair at this age. It is natural for men and women to have pubic hair. It is not a crime, a sin, something to be ashamed of, or something to be afraid of. If the pubic hair is not cleaned regularly, it can cause itching, eczema, and skin problems. We have to remove our pubic hair from time to time."

He advised Arun, "If you go to a fancy store and ask for soap to clean private areas, they will give you soap. The instructions on how to use that soap are written on it. If you still don't understand how to use it, ask your father."

@@@

The shopkeeper noticed that Arun was hesitant to come inside the fancy store. After some time, when everyone had left, he called Arun inside.

"What do you want? Why have you been lingering outside since then?", Shopkeeper asked.

"I need... I need," Arun mumbled, feeling ashamed and scared.

The shopkeeper, understanding Arun's problem, said, "Do you want soap?"

"Yes, uncle," Arun blushed.

"Why are you afraid to ask for soap? Let me tell you one thing. This is nothing to be ashamed or afraid of." He told him not to feel embarrassed, afraid, or ashamed to ask for soap in front of everyone. He asked him to use it carefully, giving him the soap.

The next day, Arun went to school early. In the evening, he led his team to victory in kabaddi. Chakri was warned by Peter sir, and Arun also asked for Chakri's forgiveness. They hugged each other.

Note: Kudos to the teachers who understand the problems of preteens and stand behind them. Teachers fill that position after parents. It should be understood that teachers have the responsibility to make children aware of such matters.

***

Voice

The boys in the street are talking crazy about the new movie that has come in theaters and the actors who have acted in it. Charan likes hero Chiranjeevi. To Munna, hero Balakrishna is life. All the boys split into two teams and argued that, 'Our hero is great, our hero is great...'

Meanwhile, Reddeppa who came from the other side asked, 'What happened? Why are you fighting?' He looked at Charan angrily.

A boy from the group complained to Reddeppa that Charan is saying, 'Balakrishna is a waste in front of Chiranjeevi's dance.'

'What's up, Chanti? Do you need all these?' Reddeppa said.

'My name is Charan not Chanti', he said sadly.

'You and that Chanti are one in my opinion,' he said sarcastically. All the boys laughed. Charan went home crying.

@@@

His uncle noticed Charan going inside the house sad and crying.

He went to Charan and asked lovingly, 'What happened? Why are you crying? Did anyone say anything?'

'There is no such thing,' he lied, tears came because of a crumb in his eye.

'Tell me the truth, did someone say something?', his uncle asked again.

He went into the room saying 'No'.

@@@

Charan sat on the bed in the room and cried. He couldn't bear to be called Chanti in front of everyone. However, he wondered why his voice sounded like a girl's voice, unlike everyone else's voice.

Reddeppa called him Chanti in front of everyone, so lately his friends and people on the street are also jokingly calling him Chanti, Chanti...

Chanti is a hijra from the same village. Reddeppa started jokingly calling Charan as Chanti...Chanti because Charan's voice is like Chanti's voice. Reddappa stays next door to Charan's house who is about thirty years old and is married.

Whenever Charan is seen, he tries to make fun of him saying Chanti... Chanti Charan is very sad because of that. He is crumbling inside. When he is alone, he cries a lot because of his voice.

@@@

Charan is 13 years old and he has a sister. Now she is studying in second class. Charan's parents work in a factory. They will go in the morning and return in the evening. There is no time for them to spend with children. Uncle and Aunt are taking care of all the children's well-being.

Uncle went to Charan's room to find out the cause of the child's pain. Charan was seen lying on one side of the bed and crying.

On seeing Charan like that, he said, 'Hey Charan, why are you crying?' He took Charan close.

After a while he said, 'Reddeppa who stays next door is calling me Chanti.'

'Because you are a child! That's why he might have called you like that, why are you crying for that?' He made a confused face.

'Chanti does not mean a child. In the evening, Chanti's sister comes wearing a saree! He is making fun of me because my voice is like Her's. Why did my voice change like this? Will I have the same voice?' Charan hugged his uncle tightly.

His uncle started explaining, "I will tell you about it, but you should not cry. All children's voices change at this age. Everyone's voice changes regardless of male or female. A strong voice emerges after months or years."

"The vocal cords of children of this age become thicker and longer. Your voice has changed because of that. It will be like this for two or three years. After that, your voice will come like my voice. This change is less noticeable in girls, but common in boys."

"Have you noticed the voice of your friends Mohan, Vishnu and Krishna has also changed. Because you are all children of the same age. Slowly everyone's voices change. Some may change quickly; others may be late. If the voice is still the same even after puberty, then there is a need to consult a doctor. But remember it's not your problem, it's natural."

"You have to be prepared for the changes in your body. It is not a strange thing or something that happens only to you. Don't cry if someone makes fun of you, instead you should answer them. If the other person is older than you, you should tell about them at home, but you should not cry inside yourself."

Charan was encouraged by his uncle to discuss such things with him even in future.

Since that day, Charan has enquired his uncle about the many changes in his body.

@@@

Charan's uncle scolded Reddappa.

Uncle was relieved to see that Charan was again talking to everyone without bothering that his voice was new and strange.

***

Periods

Telugu teacher Ram Naik's lessons are very popular among the tenth-grade students. When the teacher melodiously recites the poem, all the children attentively listen.

While singing the poem "Atajani Kanche," (A Telugu poem to the 10th standard students) loud screams were heard from the girls. Instantly, all the children gathered. Ram Naik halted his lesson and went to the children.

Tulsi had fainted, and her clothes were stained with blood. Ram Naik immediately called Sulochana teacher, who was in the next class. Sulochana helped Tulsi to the staff room.

Tulsi's friend was sent home to bring clothes. Tulsi changed her clothes and then went home. Some of the girls understood what happened to Tulsi, but the boys were not entirely aware.

For about 2 weeks, Tulsi did not attend school. The boys speculated about why Tulsi was absent. Some thought she was sick, others believed she might not be alive, and some felt it was inappropriate to discuss her illness.

@@@

"We thought Tulsi was sick! That's a lie; there was a function at her house yesterday. If she is sick, why would they have a function?" Narayana, who lives near Tulsi's house, informed the other boys.

"Tulsi isn't sick; she has become an adult woman," Seenu said cleverly.

Meanwhile, Sulochana teacher entered the classroom. She realized the boys were talking about Tulsi.

The Sulochana teacher is liked by the children. Along with her science lessons, the children eagerly listen to many new things she shares.

"What happened? Were you having a discussion about something? Why did you people stop the discussion?" she asked lovingly.

Rakesh informed Sulochana about Seenu saying something inappropriate that 'Tulsi has become an adult woman.'

The teacher, understanding the matter, said, "What's up, Seenu? Do you know what being an adult woman means?" she asked directly.

Seenu was shy and scared to speak in front of everyone.

"Do you know? Or you Don't?" she raised her voice.

"I know, ma'am, but I heard my father telling my sister not to discuss such things in front of everyone, so I can't say." He smiled shyly.

He asked Seenu to sit down and said, "Tulsi has become an adult woman. It's not something that's sick, weird, or something that no one should talk about. At this age, there are many changes in the bodies of girls, just as there are changes in the bodies of boys. A girl becoming an adult woman is called 'Adulthood.' A girl bleeds every month when she is in menstruation."

"Do you know about the uterus? The endometrium, the inner lining of the uterus, is shed and regenerated over a period of time. That discharge is called menstruation or menses. Girls may feel weak and irritable during menstruation. That's why they rest without doing any work. Tulsi also rested for a few days. In two days, she will come to school and continue her studies."

"Everyone should be aware of periods. Nothing is forbidden. We need to talk about it openly for everyone to know. There is nothing wrong with discussing it. If there are any women in your house, like your mother, sister, elder sister, sister-in-law, or aunt, who are working during their menstrual days, give them rest. Help them if you can. Speak lovingly. By doing so, there is a chance to ease their pain."

"If you still have any doubts about this, I will give you the book. It contains details about menstruation. You all should know about it in detail, not only to be informed but also to educate those who don't know."

All the children nodded their heads. Science teacher Sulochana bought and distributed the book on 'Woman Adulthood' by the famous writer Nagma Fatima, who wrote in detail about menstruation, so that children can understand it.

***

Note: It is essential to have books available in schools that provide detailed information on menstruation, changes in boys' bodies, and puberty issues. Menstruation should be openly discussed and not to be considered taboo. The topic of menstruation should be made clear not only to girls but also to boys.

Misconception

All the children were painting on the computers. The computer teacher was walking around, answering the children's questions. Meanwhile, a fight broke out between Viraj Rathod and Rajasekhar, and they ended up getting into a physical altercation.

Noticing the scuffle, the computer teacher intervened and asked the two children the reason for their fight.

"Viraj, why did the fight happen? What did you say?" the computer teacher inquired.

Viraj, looking upset, replied, "I didn't do anything, sir. The eraser on my computer isn't working properly, so I asked him to help me. But he called me Grandpa."

The computer teacher questioned Rajasekhar, "Why did you use that word?"

"I didn't say anything," Rajasekhar argued.

The computer teacher, raising his voice, asked, "Did you say that word or not?"

Viraj, with tears streaming down his face, said, "He calls me 'Grandpa' as my teeth fell out, and tells everyone that my mouth stinks, instructing them not to talk to me."

@@@

"If the teeth are falling out, it shouldn't be a reason to call someone 'Grandpa.' Everyone here will lose their teeth eventually. I also lost my teeth when I was your age. Now look at them; they're in great shape," Computer teacher said, showing his beautiful row of teeth.

"Many people do not get teeth right after birth. Some people get it but it is a very small percentage. At six months of birth, teeth start coming in. Those teeth are 'Milk-teeth', but they aren't firm, so we lose them after a certain age. New and strong teeth grow in their place, which are 'Permanent teeth'. Teeth don't come and go all at once. Some teeth come out first, and slowly, as we become adults, a total of 32 permanent teeth will emerge," he further explained.

To maintain beautiful teeth and avoid gaps between them, you should brush well every morning. Improper brushing can lead to plaque buildup between the teeth, food stuck in the mouth, and gum problems, which in turn leads to Bad odor from the mouth.

"Not only that, the brush you use should be soft and not stiff. Don't brush your teeth too hard; brush slowly, up and down, following a method. Otherwise, your gums may get damaged and bleed, causing bad breath. If possible, brush again for two minutes before going to bed at night. If you still have a bad smell from your mouth, inform your parents and visit a doctor," he advised.

The computer teacher reassured the children that losing teeth doesn't mean they won't get them back. He emphasized that if any friends are dealing with bad breath, it's essential to express care and love rather than speaking negatively.

Turning to Rajasekhar, the teacher said, "Rajasekhar, apologize to Viraj." The two children hugged each other lovingly and apologized.

The computer teacher then approached Viraj, who was still upset, and checked to see if there was really a bad smell coming from his mouth.

@@@

Computer teacher called Viraj's parents the next day, and recounted the events of the previous day.

He explained to his parents, "These incidents can have a detrimental impact on a child's self-esteem. Viraj is an excellent student, but unfortunately, he has been dealing with this issue for quite some time now! If not you, then who will take care of the little problems children face? It's crucial to understand that what may seem like a small issue to us can be a significant problem for children. Ensure you use a good toothbrush and toothpaste. Let me explain the proper brushing technique. Recognize that it's the parents' responsibility to identify and address their child's problems early on."

"Absolutely, sir! We didn't realize the severity of the issue. We will switch Viraj's toothbrush and toothpaste immediately. If the problem persists, we'll take him to the doctor," assured Viraj's father.

@@@

After a week, the computer teacher felt a deep sense of satisfaction seeing Viraj's teeth shining brightly. Rajasekhar, Viraj happily painted on the computer.

***

Note: Many children hold the misconception that lost teeth will not grow back. It is our responsibility to clarify that this is not true. Additionally, bad breath is not solely a concern for children but also for adults. If left unaddressed, children may struggle to solve the issue. We should stand by them in such matters. It's crucial to ensure that misconceptions and problems do not hinder the growth of children.

A Natural Discomfort

"Did you notice? our Mayank is irritable, impatient, and worried these days," Meenakshi informed her husband, Venkateswara Rao.

"Yes? Could you sense what's going on?" he replied, glancing at his wife while working.

"Will he tell me? Ask and see for yourself," Venkateswara Rao observed the pain on Meenakshi's face.

"I will talk, don't worry," he reassured his wife, offering her courage.

@@@

Mayank is sixteen years old. He excels in his studies and has a passion for singing. He often participates in small stage shows. His parents, in accordance with his wishes, have made all the necessary arrangements for him to pursue music.

Mayank has a younger brother in the sixth standard and a sister in the third standard. Despite being this young, Mayank has already gained fame through his singing, even securing an opportunity to sing in a Telugu movie. Meenakshi, his mother, became concerned as such a talented and accomplished boy seemed irritable and worried.

Both of Mayank's parents are highly responsible in their approach to raising their children. Venkateswara Rao believes in being friends with the children rather than just acting as parents.

@@@

Venkateswara Rao took the children to Park, which was a little far away. Mayank's younger brother and sister were engrossed in playing. As Mayank and Venkateswara Rao walked forward, Venkateswara Rao tried to understand the reason for Mayank's concern.

"Is everything alright at school?" Venkateswara Rao asked,

attempting to address the topic gently.

"Everything is fine, father!" Mayank looked confused, not understanding why his father had asked.

"Is there something you want to talk about?" his father asked directly.

"Nothing, dad," Mayank replied, visibly worried.

"Your mother mentioned that you've been feeling irritable," Venkateswara Rao said, placing his hand lovingly on Mayank's shoulder and assuring him that he could share if there was any problem.

Mayank was unsure of how to express his concerns to his father, despite knowing that his father was understanding and caring.

"You can tell me anything. Don't be afraid or shy," reassured Venkateswara Rao.

After a moment of hesitation, Mayank finally spoke, "I've noticed some changes in my body, and it's making me feel embarrassed, especially in the morning. It's awkward when it happens at school, on stage, and around others."

Understanding the cause of Mayank's pain, fear, anxiety, irritation, and concern, Venkateswara Rao hugged him lovingly. He aimed to ease the tension, by conveying that there was nothing wrong, with a caring and responsible hug.

"Didn't I tell you to ask me if you have any doubts or concerns? There's no need to be so tense about such a small matter."

"The natural occurrence of an erection in men is termed 'involuntary erections.' It occurs even when a person is not thinking anything sexually, and there is no deliberate involvement. This is a normal and natural thing that happens to most men, not just at your age. If it happens, it means that you are healthy."

"Hormones fluctuate, mainly due to changes in the testosterone hormone. It's normal to experience this two or three times a day. It's not a health problem, and you should not feel embarrassed about it. Understand that it's not your fault."

"If it happens when there are other people around, try to use your school bag to cover, adjust your pants discreetly, focus on another task, avoid moving, and refrain from touching. If it happens at home, a cold shower is sufficient. Don't worry that someone is watching and thinking negatively. It is not a crime, harmful, sick, or wrong."

"Don't be so irritable and anxious from now on. If there's any trouble, you have to tell me, okay!" Venkateswara Rao lovingly kissed Mayank's forehead.

Mayank hugged his father tightly, feeling blessed to have such a supportive father.

@@@

Afterward, Meenakshi was overjoyed to see Mayank happy and cheerful.

***

Short

As soon as the interval bell rang, all the children went down and ran to the ground. Some of them were pushing and fighting to buy chocolates found in the shop.

Raju, Umesh and Nagarjuna went to the washroom. They stood in a row and urinated.

'Hey! Let's all three pee together at the same time. The winner is the one whose urine goes higher on the wall,' said Raju.

Umesh, Nagarjuna agreed to the competition and urinated. Umesh passed urine higher than the other two, Nagarjuna took the next place but Raju's urine did not fall too high on the wall. With that, Umesh and Nagarjuna made fun of Raju.

They said that yours is short because there is something wrong with you.

@@@

Raju's father does agriculture, Mother is a homemaker. Raju also has two younger sisters. Three are studying in the same school.

Raju's father's idea was to educate the children no matter how difficult it was. Accordingly, three children study well.

Because of the words of friends, the other day, Raju's heart started to tremble. 'Why is mine so short? It would be a shame if the rest of his friends knew about it,' he thought.

He stopped eating, reading and playing while always thinking about it. Raju's father noticed that he was sitting there gloomily, always thinking.

'What happened? Why are you sitting here?' he asked lovingly.

He just said, 'I'm fine.'

Raju is very fond of his grandfather. Grandfather also likes Raju too. Raju's father told his grandfather about Raju.

@@@

Seeing Raju silently sitting on the block in front of the house, the grandfather went to Raju.

'What's up little one? What are you thinking about?', asked the grandfather.

'Nothing Grandfather,' he replied.

"Are you trying to hide something from me? Tell me what is the cause of your pain and anxiety," Grandfather asked again lovingly, and told him that he would solve the problem.

'Well, can I ask you something?'

'You can ask any number of questions,' Grandpa replied, kissing Raju on the cheek.

"Umesh, Nagarjuna and I are studying in the same class! Moreover, everyone is the same age. But why am I the only one who is short and skinny?" He explained the whole thing to his grandfather.

'Oh! That is why my Raju is sad.' He started saying, 'Listen carefully.'

"In order to grow strong and tall, you need to eat nutritious food. Not only that but also play well and rest. If the body does not get the required nutrition at the right time and age, the children will not grow properly."

"Genes are also one of the reasons why some children do not grow taller even if they eat well, play and exercise, that means if your mother and father are short. Moreover, no one in our house is very tall, so you did not get taller. There are many other reasons besides this."

"All you have to do is eat well, play, exercise and rest. Keeping that aside, let me answer your second question."

"As the body ages, the organs grow. Some people grow all their limbs quickly. For others, it is a bit slower. There is no difference between small and big. Whether it is small or big it works the same way."

"Your friends may be getting urine with pressure when you compete. Besides, they are taller than you, so they urinate high on the wall."

"Do not do such things. Remember, don't feel bad that your penis is small. However, size does not depend on height. Some are tall but their penis is short. Others are short and thin but their penis is large. It depends on the changes in their body."

"Tell me if you have any problems with urination. If you really have any problem, I will take you to the doctor."

@@@

Raju shared what he learned from his grandfather with his friends. Umesh and Nagarjuna apologized to Raju. They were relieved to find answers to their doubts.

After that, the three are engaged in games and studies together.

***

Note: We all have a responsibility to understand children's pain and answer their doubts, problems and misconceptions.

Identity

Shiva's father Ramakrishna owns a bicycle shop and Mother works as a mason by day. Both the parents are working hard to educate Shiva. No matter how many people say that if Shiva is employed, the financial situation will improve, they prefer to educate Shiva.

Ramakrishna believes that their lives are like this because of their lack of education and that they would have had a better life if they had been educated.

Shiva completed his tenth standard. After getting the results, he wanted to join the diploma.

Shiva is tall and beautiful. Friends joke that if you were born as a girl, we would have married you. Their words did not hurt Shiva. He used to laugh out loud when someone said that.

@@@

Ever since his conception, Shiva loves dressing up like a woman and wearing a saree. He used to wear his mother's saree when his parents were not at home. He used to look in the mirror and cringe.

He is sad and afraid of having such thoughts. He could not understand why he had such thoughts and desires, unlike other boys.

Boys are naturally attracted to girls and girls are naturally attracted to boys. But Shiva gets attracted towards boys.

@@@

One day, when both the parents were not at home, he locked the door and wore his mother's saree and put a blob on his face. He sat in a corner covering his face with hands and wept bitterly. There were bangles on his hands and anklets on legs.

Shiva did not open the door even after his parents knocked on the door many times. After about ten minutes, Shiva opened the door in a panic. He opened the door without removing the blob on his face and the bangles on his hands in fear of his parents coming.

On seeing Shiva, Vijaya, mother wept bitterly and said, 'You are evil in my stomach. Why are you doing this? What will happen if anyone knows about this in the village?' She hit his cheeks.

Ramakrishna stopped his wife and said, 'Let's put him in a hostel in Kadapa. If he stays in the village, not only will we be humiliated but also his education will be destroyed.'

He consoled his wife by saying that if he concentrates on his studies, he will stop doing these activities.

@@@

As expected, Shiva was admitted to Diploma College in Kadapa and placed in a hostel.

But the feelings in Shiva's mind did not die. He could not stop his thoughts, and started to get visible in life-style.

All his friends in college started calling him hijra. He could not read properly when everyone said so. He wondered why he was born like that. The Physics Lecturer came to know that the children were addressing Shiva as Hijra.

One day, while he was in class, the physics lecturer heard Murali saying to Shiva, 'Hey hijra' don't sit next to me'.

Physics lecturer observed that and warned Murali to apologize to Shiva. And he said that...,

"Like Men and women, hijras and other races are also human beings. They should not be called so mean and bad. The words hijra,

Point5 hurt them a lot. As we age, our body changes. Also, there are changes in thoughts when entering adulthood. Desires, likes and dislikes arise."

"Some think that they should be like girls and vice versa. It is not a disease. Also, some boys get attracted towards boys and girls get attracted towards girls. It should be remembered that this is all a matter of their choice."

"Everyone has their own choice and we should respect that. And it is wrong to trouble others for their choice. There are many people like Shiva in the society. We should not insult such people; we should invite them."

The physics lecturer told all the children that they should never talk to Shiva like that again in a derisive, sarcastic, derogatory way.

@@@

After the class, the physics lecturer said to Shiva, 'tell me if anyone bothers you. Let me meet your parents once if possible.'

A few days later Shiva's parents met the physics lecturer.

He explained Shiva's in detail that, "there is nothing wrong with Shiva, you should not be afraid. There are many such people in the society. At this age, if Shiva is treated differently, he will lose his respect and dignity and his life will be destroyed."

"Whether our child is a boy, a girl, a Hijra or anything else, we should love them. If you don't understand them, then how will someone else? Shiva is the topper in the class. He will be in a very high position if he has your encouragement and love. Give him the freedom and courage to make his choice."

"Children fully understand who they are while they are growing. At this stage they have many doubts, misconceptions and problems. It is difficult for society to understand people like Shiva so you as a parent should love and support more."

"Shiva yearns for this society to recognize him as a woman. There is nothing wrong with that. Please give a chance to Shiva on how he wanted to be."

Ramakrishna hugged Shiva tightly. Shiva's mother also took Shiva close and kissed him.

Shiva was celebrated as if he had conquered the world.

***

Note: Children begin to come to know about themselves when puberty begins. Adults should first understand that 'gender identity' is a personal matter, then tell the children to understand. This is one of the major changes that come with puberty. The child struggles to understand this change. At that time, if the parents and the society distance themselves, they will be the ones who have ruined their life unjustly.

Children are not the possessions or rights of parents. Society should give them the freedom to be in whatever identity they like.

Dissatisfaction

Around fifty children of class nine and ten students studying at Harvard International School went on a tour to Ooty. Six teachers accompanied them. They stayed in a hotel near the botanical garden in Ooty.

Some children were enjoying the cool weather and the beauty of nature. The teachers warned the children who were still in their rooms to wake up and get ready early.

All the rooms were crowded. Vinod wore new clothes, applied some cream on his face, and combed his hair well. Vinod is very handsome and charming, often referred to as Cupid.

He is tall, strong, smiling, pleasant, and smart. Vinod expresses what he feels in his heart on face. He strives to keep those around him happy and lively.

@@@

Vinod and Harsha are studying in class X. Harsha excels in academics compared to Vinod. However, Vinod prioritizes his physique over his studies. He believes that no one in the school is more handsome than him.

Harsha harbors a dislike for Vinod. In reality, Harsha feels hurt by anyone who appears prettier, taller, or stronger than him. Since the age of ten, Harsha has been experiencing feelings of anger, disgust, irritation, boredom, and dislike towards himself, impacting his ability to focus on studies.

Struggling with a breakout of pimples on his face, Harsha perceives himself as unattractive, assuming that no one wants to talk to him. Recently, his confidence has been decreasing, feeling unhappy about not being as handsome, tall, fair-complexioned, and strong as Vinod.

Deeply dissatisfied with his body, Harsha always complains about his nose, lips, height, and color not being right. Despite using beauty products to enhance his appearance, he is disappointed with the lack of results.

@@@

All the children got ready and left for Doddabetta peak in Ooty. Vinod, in particular, received admiration from the other children, causing Harsha to feel increasingly dissatisfied. The jealousy and envy that had been brewing in his mind surfaced. While all the children were enjoying themselves, Harsha appeared lonely, apathetic, and avoided interacting with anyone.

The social teacher noticed Harsha's mood and approached him, asking, 'What happened, Harsha? Why are you so moody?'

Harsha replied, 'Nothing, ma'am,' showing no joy on his face.

The teacher advised, 'Look! All your friends are happily enjoying themselves. Why are you alone like this? We shouldn't be alone when we are with everyone. Is there any problem?'

Harsha simply responded, 'No, ma'am,' and reluctantly joined the other children.

@@@

After finishing the tour and reaching home, the social teacher met Harsha's parents.

She expressed her concern, saying, "Harsha studies well but always seems to be unhappy about something. He is unable to talk to anyone due to his unhappiness and is now unable to pay attention to studies. Do you know what is the cause of his pain?"

Harsha's father responded, "He is very intelligent, but he is thinking stupidly about one thing. I have said a lot, but he doesn't pay any heed. The main reason for his unhappiness is the feeling that he is not handsome."

Continuing, he said, "I have given him many medicines to grow taller and whiter, but there is no result. No matter how much you say that beauty is not important for a human, he should have good character, but it still affects. My wife is crying because of this, what shall we do?"

The social teacher understood the reason for Harsha's pain and dissatisfaction. She called Harsha to her room while his parents were present.

She explained to him, "What's bothering you, Harsha? I thought you were very intelligent, but I did not think you would think so naively. Who said you are not handsome? Handsomeness has no measure."

"Many changes occur in the body at this age. And I understand it is natural for children of your age to think that they should have a nose like this, a mouth like this, their color is not like others, and wonder why my voice is not like them."

"It is common to feel dissatisfied with your body. Experiencing too much pain, anger, and impatience because your body is not growing the way you like and want is not healthy for you. Try to find contentment with what you have instead of longing for what you don't have."

"No one is perfect when it comes to beauty. Every human being has some flaws. Understand that there is no flawless person in this world. Instead of worrying that your body is not beautiful, focus on keeping your mind beautiful."

"Comparing yourself to someone else's will not allow you to move forward. From now on, pay attention to your studies and your life."

@@@

"Look! The main reason for Harsha to think like that is his age. At this age, such thoughts, dissatisfaction, depression, and confusion are natural."

"Encourage him to focus on his strengths and favorite things rather than his weaknesses and dissatisfactions. Avoid responding with anger, rage, hitting, or cursing. Many individuals feel like Harsha during this age. It is a very common thing that happens in adolescence. After this stage, everything will settle itself," she further explained to his parent's.

@@@

After two months, the social teacher came to know that Harsha was learning to play the guitar and asked him to showcase his skills. Harsha played the guitar smartly, intelligently, and with great joy.

Along with Vinod, all the children in the class clapped and congratulated Harsha. Harsha understood then that talent, kindness, a good personality, and good character are more important than beauty.

***

Note: It is natural for children to experience dissatisfaction with their bodies as they enter adolescence. Parents should understand that and support them.

Fickle

Saptagiri and Anuradha have two sons. The elder son is named Narahari, and the younger one is named Sai. After fifth grade Sai had to discontinue his studies.

Saptagiri also advised Narahari to quit school and start working, but Narahari expressed his desire to continue his education. Despite initial resistance, Narahari was eventually enrolled in a government school.

Narahari is now doing well in his studies, but he has a strong desire to rejoin his younger brother in pursuing education. However, Sai, due to family circumstances, is currently working with his parents.

Saptagiri and Anuradha work as agricultural labor, and their livelihood depends on it. If they cease working, it would become challenging for the family to secure food.

@@@

'Harikrishna, Praveen, Vishnuvardhan, Manoj, and Gopal come from wealthier families. They live in large houses and have the means to acquire whatever they desire. However, I lack a home, face financial challenges, and struggle to ensure we have enough food to eat,' Narahari thought.

The sight of anyone, whether at school or on the street, triggers a persistent feeling in Narahari's mind—wondering why I can't have a life like theirs. Unlike my friends, I am plagued by thoughts about how to improve our financial situation.

The growing desire and hope to live a life comparable to others have intensified in Narahari. There's a strong urge to find ways to earn money and improve their circumstances.

@@@

With such thoughts and facing numerous difficulties, Narahari managed to complete the tenth standard.

However, due to financial constraints, Saptagiri couldn't afford to enroll him in intermediate education. But Narahari adamantly declared his willingness to continue studying.

Feeling ashamed that he had to work while his friends were pursuing further education, Narahari engaged in a heated argument with his parents. In the midst of the conflict, Saptagiri resorted to physical punishment and harsh words, expressing his frustration and regret about having a son like Narahari. This provoked anger and fury in Narahari.

Feeling dissatisfied towards his father, Narahari left the house quietly one night while everyone was asleep.

@@@

Not knowing where to go or what to do after leaving home, Narahari found it difficult to endure hunger. Fueled by resentment towards his parents and society, he harbored troubling thoughts. Sleeping on the streets, he consumed whatever food he could find.

Concerned about their missing child, Saptagiri and Anuradha reported the matter to the police. Two days later, the police located Narahari. Upon seeing him, Anuradha burst into tears, Saptagiri went out of his way to beat up Narahari before the police intervened and stopped him.

Expressing his anger and frustration, Narahari shouted at his father.

Seeing this, the police then took the initiative to arrange counseling sessions for both Narahari and Saptagiri.

@@@

Counseling was provided to address the problems, doubts, misconceptions, and concerns of young children.

Dr. Dasari Ramana had an exclusive conversation with Narahari, delving into his thoughts, ambitions, and the reasons that led him to leave home.

He emphasized to Narahari that whatever parents do, they do it for the well-being of their children. He stressed that it is wrong to fight and oppose his parents, without thinking about family circumstances.

While acknowledging that it's natural for someone his age to feel the need to achieve something, he advised Narahari that success requires talent and thoughtful planning, not impulsiveness or anger.

He encouraged Narahari to think carefully, plan effectively, and work hard to improve his family's financial situation. He further highlighted the importance of diligent effort in achieving one's goals, cautioning against hasty decisions that could not only harm Narahari but also impact his family.

Dr. Dasari Ramana then called Saptagiri and Anuradha into the room to hear their perspective on the situation.

After hearing them he said, "See, Saptagiri, Narahari is young. His mind is very impressionable, and he's grappling with some thoughts. However, this is not a disease or illness. It's typical for children of this age to have such thoughts. They often feel like they don't fit in with others, and it's important for us to understand that."

"When dealing with children who have reached this age, it's crucial to speak to them with love rather than being rude, angry, or furious."

"Communication should be delivered slowly and with understanding. Children at this age have their own thoughts and desires, and simply telling them what they must do may not be effective. Instead, it's important to listen to them as well."

"If children are going astray, it's better to guide them lovingly rather than resorting to hitting, shouting, or cursing. The way you have adapted is not conducive to effective communication. If you further provoke children without recognizing that these behaviors are part of their age-related development, you risk negatively impacting their lives."

"I am willing to provide the necessary financial support for both children's education. Please ensure they receive a good education."

With that, Saptagiri, Anuradha, and Dr. Ramana extended their conversation. The police officers also pledged financial assistance for Narahari's education.

@@@

Narahari was enrolled in Intermediate, while Sai continued attending school. Saptagiri and Anuradha made a firm decision to work even harder to ensure their children received an education. Recognizing the importance of maintaining a positive and supportive environment, Saptagiri resolved not to misbehave with the children.

***

Note: A young child's mind is fickle. It is essential not to react with anger, fury, or lash out when trying to communicate with them. From the age of nine until they are teenagers, children should be raised with care. During this period, their ideas know no bounds, and it is crucial for adults to recognize that these behaviors are part of the natural developmental effects of their age.

Digital Identity

For two months, Amar has been persistently pleading for a phone, arguing that all his friends own one and he desires to have his own mobile too.

His father, Pratapa Subbarayudu, responded emphasizing the importance of studying well and achieving good marks in his exams rather than considering the purchase of a phone.

Despite this, Amar resorted to a drastic measure—he stopped eating until he was provided with a phone.

Unable to bear his son's suffering, Pratapa Subbarayudu eventually gave in and bought Amar a mobile phone. However, he imposed a condition: Amar could use the phone for only one hour a day.

Amar, complying with the condition, dedicated his phone time to social media platforms like Facebook, WhatsApp, and YouTube.

Initially, he posted photos on Facebook which received minimal response. In an attempt to garner attention, Amar started sharing details about his daily life at home on Facebook.

However, he became disheartened as he still received little response. Frustrated, he started posting photos related to home situations every evening. He eagerly checked his phone every five minutes for likes and comments.

Pratapa Subbarayudu eventually stopped monitoring Amar's phone usage.

Amar, however, became increasingly consumed by the desire for more likes and comments on his photos and videos on Facebook.

Seeking advice from a friend, he started creating short videos in a desperate attempt to gain recognition, battling feelings of anger, impatience, and pain at not being acknowledged despite his efforts.

In any case, Amar's ultimate goal was to achieve popularity by receiving more likes and comments on his Facebook content.

After all of this, Amar made a decision. One night, he viewed various famous photos and videos. He posted a picture with just underwear, thinking it would go viral and gain recognition.

Within a few hours, there were numerous likes and comments. Many of them criticized Amar, while some praised it as very good.

The next day, Amar's father learned about the photo posted by Amar.

He took the phone from Amar, beat him, cursed at him, and shouted loudly, expressing his disappointment that Amar had brought shame to their family in the village.

Acknowledging his mistake, Amar admitted, "What I did was wrong. I don't get likes and comments when I post photos normally. That's why I did it," explaining his misguided attempt to seek attention and recognition.

"If you don't get likes, will you post photos without clothes? Have you lost your mind? Did I give you the phone for all this?", his father scolded him.

He promised his father that he would not do that again, but he soon resumed using the phone. This time, he posted nude photos and videos using a fake name instead of his own.

Amar completely lost interest in his studies. He constantly walked around holding his phone, neglecting even going out to play.

Pratapa Subbarayudu grew suspicious and checked the phone while Amar slept.

Upon discovering Amar posting photos and videos with a fake profile, he lamented that his son was spoiled. He shared the matter with his nephew, who is studying in the city, knowing that beating and scolding would not solve the problem.

Pratapa Subbarayudu's Nephew advised him to immediately bring Amar to the city. After a few days, he took Amar and went to the city.

@@@

Amar was taken to a psychologist. The doctor spoke to Amar separately and understood the problem.

"The mobile should not be used excessively. It is inappropriate to use social media under a name other than our own. Moreover, one should not do such things to become popular on social media. There Should be a limit for everything. If you behave beyond that, it will be difficult to succeed in life. Remember, recognition should come through your talent, not through inappropriate means like this," he explained.

The doctor also had a separate conversation with Pratapa Subbarayudu.

"This is not a mental or medical illness. Children of this age naturally seek a 'Digital Identity,' especially those who use social media."

"The percentage of children committing suicide because they do not receive likes and comments, feeling unnoticed, is increasing. Additionally, there is a growing tendency to believe that what is portrayed on social media is true. Children of this age are particularly susceptible to such influences."

"Medicines may not be effective in curing Amar. It is suggested to create free time for him, encouraging activities he enjoys, whether it's learning games, music, or anything he likes.

Minimize phone usage as much as possible. Instead of resorting to cursing, hitting, or excessive shouting, communicate with him calmly."

@@@

Pratapa Subbarayudu's nephew gifted books to Amar. Consequently, Amar developed a habit of reading books and playing games.

Unlike before, Amar's parents began spending more time with him, engaging in meaningful conversations. Amar shared his thoughts on the topics covered in the books he had read.

Amar was finally born out of the desire to have a digital identity.

***

Note: Digital identity exists in most people but is more prevalent in preteens. There is a risk that it may lead children astray. We all share the responsibility of ensuring that children do not become victims of it.

Privacy

Malla Reddy and Bhaskar Rao have been living on the same street for ten years. Malla Reddy has two children: the older one is twelve years old, and the younger one is eight years old. Bhaskar Rao has a son and a daughter.

Malla Reddy's eldest son and Bhaskar Rao's son attend the same school and share a good friendship.

Malla Reddy struggles with a quick temper, anger, and rage. He holds a firm belief that his children should follow his instructions without question.

Despite Chandrakala, his wife, advising him not to be overly strict with their growing children, Malla Reddy remains unyielding. He is determined to enforce a disciplined upbringing, ensuring his children do not cross the boundaries he sets.

@@@

Malla Reddy's son's name is Vihan, and Bhaskar Rao's son's name is Kiansh. Both went to play football in the evening.

On their way back home after playing football, Kiansh asked Vihan, 'Shall we go to the cinema on Sunday?'

Vihan replied, 'If I go to the movies, my father will beat me. Whenever I sit in my room looking at the mobile for a while, he growls loudly. He is always behind me like a shadow at home. Even if I am in the washroom for a long time, he bangs on the door.'

'If I am talking to someone on the phone, he will turn on the speaker. He asks to talk for a while. If someone calls, he will talk first. In fact, my life has become devoid of privacy' he shared his pain with his friend.

"My mom and dad don't behave like that. They give me and my sister the required privacy. I am friends with my father. I am lucky to be his son," says Kiansh happily.

Vihan is hurt by Kiansh's words. He wishes he had a father like that.

@@@

Kiansh tells his parents about Vihan's pain, expressing, 'I am very lucky to have parents like you.'

Bhaskar Rao understands Vihan's situation and decides to talk to Malla Reddy about the matter.

Two days later, Malla Reddy and Bhaskar Rao meet outside the house after dinner.

Malla Reddy asks Bhaskar Rao, 'What are the children doing?'.

Bhaskar Rao responded, 'They are watching a new movie together on the phone.'

Malla Reddy expresses concern, 'What! movies at this time? Moreover, if children are given a phone and left alone like that, they will be spoiled.'

Bhaskar Rao, who was waiting for the right moment, seized this opportunity.

"Growing children have certain likes and desires. We should not intervene in every little thing. As parents, while we make tough decisions in the case of children, we do not have the right to take away their likes, desires, and privacy," he said directly.

"Nonsense! Do you want to leave the children to the wind? Look at how society is!" Malla Reddy retorted without valuing Bhaskara Rao's words at all.

"Is it good to not believe our children? Doubting children in every small thing is not a part of a good up-bringing process. Everything has a limit. If we act beyond that limit, children will become our enemies. Children entering puberty desire some privacy. You can explain the pros and cons, but it is not a good idea to meddle in everything," Bhaskar Rao further explained.

"We should trust our children. The mind is restless in youth. The brain is confused when it does not understand many things. We should support and guide them rather than scaring them. How can a bird fly if its wings are folded?"

Children should be allowed to fly and be free. Their privacy should not be violated. He emphatically stated that children should be given the required amount of freedom and privacy.

Understanding Bhaskar Rao's words, Malla Reddy remained silent.

@@@

From that day, he started showing more love towards the two children, refraining from being suspicious or disturbing their privacy.

Vihan celebrated the change in his father. He strongly believed that he should not do anything that would trouble his parents or break the trust they showed in him.

***

Note: It is not a good practice to tie the wings of growing children and deprive them of privacy.

Testicles

Like every day, when Hari went home from school, he cleaned his feet, hands, and face before going to play for a while. There is a Shiva temple near the house, and all the children play there in the evening.

Hari reached home tired after playing games like Kho-Kho and Kabaddi. As soon as he stepped into the house, Ramadevi, his mother, instructed him to go and take a bath.

Hari went into the washroom to take a bath.

@@@

Hari is the beloved son of Ramadevi and Somasekhar. He was born very late after their marriage, so he is being brought up in a carefree manner.

Hari's father works in an electricity office. Until four years ago, Ramadevi worked as a teacher in a private school, now she is only handling home.

@@@

He examined his entire body while taking the bath. For one year he has been observing many changes in his body.

Lately, sweat and a particular smell are coming from the body. Somasekhar told Hari to clean the sensitive parts well. That's why he took utmost care of his testicles while cleaning his body.

But when he noticed his testicles, one was small and the other was large. Hari felt scared and confused. He bathed in fear and came out. Meanwhile, his father also reached home from the office. Noticing his son's agitation, he inquired about what had happened.

Hari remained silent and did not give the reason for his confusion.

Somasekhar thought that it is not good to ask again and again, as children's moods change with age, and if there is any problem, he will tell.

@@@

Hari was not talking, not eating well for two days. He seemed distracted and scared. His parents realized something was bothering their son.

Taking Hari into the room, Somasekhar lovingly asked what happened. 'No matter what, your dad will fix it,' he assured.

Hari put on a tearful face and told his father what he had observed while taking the bath.

Somasekhar took Hari to the washroom and examined the testicles. He explained, 'that there is nothing to be afraid of; testicles grow quickly in children of this age. Naturally, one of them is up and the other down, and for some, the two can be equal.'

After his father told him that it was not a problem, Hari gained some confidence. However, Somasekhar understood something is still hidden in some corner of his mind.

The next day, Somasekhar took Hari to the hospital.

Hari told the doctor that there was a lot of sweat and some kind of smell coming from his body.

The doctor explained, "At this age, due to changes in hormones, the body releases more sweat and odor. That's not a problem. However, the body should always be kept clean to avoid skin diseases. If possible, you should bathe twice a day."

After examining Hari, the doctor reassured him, "Your testicles are normal, and there is no such thing as big or small as you think. If one is a bit down, like your dad said, there's no problem." Hari breathed a sigh of relief upon hearing that.

The doctor prescribed medicine to prevent itching and smell.

***

Note: If the testicles are painful, swollen, or if one is significantly larger than the other, there is a possibility of a problem. The purpose of this story is to encourage you not to be too afraid. Consulting a doctor is better than self-medication.

Stress

Srinivas Yadav and Bhavani have two children. Srinivas Yadav owns a five-acre farm, primarily cultivating chili. Bhavani also helps with the farm work while taking care of the household chores.

The eldest son's name is Chandu. He studied in Telugu medium until the tenth standard and then joined Intermediate in English Medium. The younger son is currently in the ninth standard.

As there was no intermediate college in the village, Chandu was admitted to Rajampet.

@@@

Chandu, who studied in the village until class 10th, found hostel life scary and disturbing. Additionally, being new to English medium for Intermediate studies, he faced challenges understanding the lectures.

He informed his parents that he couldn't comprehend what the lecturers were saying, and even found the food unsatisfactory.

'I admitted you to college after taking out a loan. If you come back home, we will lose respect in the village,' Srinivas Yadav angrily responded. He emphasized that Chandu should somehow complete the two years.

Feeling unheard by his father, Chandu confided in his mother, expressing his frustration.

'If you complete two years, you will have a good life. How can you be happy in life if you don't work hard?' His mother pleaded with chandu to listen to his father.

After expressing his feelings for a few months, Chandu eventually stopped sharing with his parents, feeling they wouldn't understand.

@@@

Chandu, who was accustomed to lovingly cooked meals by his mother at home, did not appreciate the hostel meals. Consequently, he struggled to eat the hostel food.

Despite his best efforts, he found it challenging to comprehend the lessons, and the hostel environment felt like a prison to him. His performance in the first internal exams was very poor.

The college staff sent a message to Chandu's parents, urging them to come immediately.

Upon seeing Chandu, Bhavani experienced a mix of emotions.

She pleaded with her husband not to let Chandu stay there for even a moment, urging to take him home immediately.

After careful consideration, Srinivas Yadav decided to take Chandu home for four days and then drop him back at the college.

They emphasized to Chandu that if he didn't focus on his studies, his life would be ruined, and he would be leading a life like them.

Despite their warnings, when Chandu did not listen, Srinivas Yadav resorted to hitting and cursing him. Bhavani intervened, preventing Chandu from being hit further.

Srinivas Yadav, feared that his son's life would be adversely affected without education. He worried about the potential insults and gossip in the village.

@@@

Feeling depressed because his parents couldn't understand him, Chandu cried with no one to share his pain. Underwhelmed with loneliness, he reached a point of despair. In the solitude of the night, after everyone had gone to sleep, he consumed the insecticide that was typically used for crops.

Chandu was taken to the hospital, after getting to know the matter, when he cried loudly that his stomach was hurting. He narrowly escaped death.

He was discharged from the hospital two days later.

The entire village came to see Chandu. Relatives of Srinivas and Bhavani also visited. Chandu was encouraged to be brave, while parents were reprimanded.

Srinivas Yadav's elder brother was deeply upset with him. He emphasized that children of this age are sensitive and that they need love rather than physical punishment. He questioned who could truly understand the pain and suffering of children if not their parents.

He also emphasized that growing children cannot handle excessive pressure and stress, especially during adolescence. He urged everyone to consider that academics are not everything in life.

'Is facing shame in the village worse than losing a child? Even if honor is lost, it can be regained. However, can the lost child be brought back?' He stressed the importance of trying to be loving and understanding with the children.

"If you take such steps in life for small things, huge problems may arise in life. How will you solve and cope with them?" He explained and advised Chandu to be brave.

@@@

Srinivas Yadav acknowledged his mistake and enrolled Chandu to an intermediate college in the next town.

Chandu attended college from home and dedicated himself to his studies. Srinivas Yadav started understanding Chandu better.

Chandu made a promise to his father that he would not contemplate suicide again. Through this experience, Chandu learned that no matter how challenging life becomes, one can endure and fight through difficulties, and death is not the solution.

***

Note: Children are typically very sensitive, and their minds are particularly delicate at a young age. Adults should recognize that sensitivity is a natural effect of their age, and it is not advisable to impose excessive pressure on children.

Published Books

Poetry:
- Akhilaasha
- Viplava Suryudu
- Nakshatra Jallulu
- Burada Navvindi
- Mattinaipotaanu (A volume of travel poetry)
- Gayala Nundi Padyala Daaka
- Paraka

Long Poems:
- "Y"- Long poem on 'Hijra' Community.
- Oori Madhyalo Bodrai- First Telugu long poem on 'Female Organ'.

Story Volume:
- Shuru- Rayalaseema Dialect Muslim Minority Stories.

Novels:
- Madi Datani Mata- First Telugu Novel on 'Gay' Community.
- Ranku- Muslim Minority Telugu Novel on 'Illicit Relationships'.
- Devudi Bharya- A Novel on the 'Devadasi' System.

Literary Criticism:
- Vivechani- A Volume of Fifty Criticism Essays.
- Akademi Aanimuthyalu- Essays on Kendra Sahitya Akademi award-winning books.
- Kavitva Swaram- Criticism Essays on Modern Telugu Poetry.

Hindi:
- Zindagi Ke Heere (Nanos in Hindi)- The first book to introduce Nanos to Hindi literature.

Children's literature:
- Papodu - Rayalaseema Dialect Children's Literature Stories focusing solely on children's issues.
- Balasahityamloki - Criticism Essays on Children's Literature.
- Balala Hakkulu - First Telugu Children's Novel on Children's Rights.

Translation:
- Tiny Treasures - Children Stories translated from Telugu to English. Published by 'Ukiyoto publishing house.'

Editor:
- Matrusparsha - Poems are written on Mother by 160 poets.
- Tadi Leni Goodu - Collection of pratilipi story event winning stories.

Awards:

For Books:
- 'Y'- Shakuntala Jaini Smaraka Kala Puraskar.
- Vivechani- Sahitya Akademi Yuva Puraskar-2023.

For Writer:
- 'Kavi Mitra' Award from Satrayagam Sahitya Vedika.
- 'Katha Bharathi' Puraskar from Pratilipi Website.
- 'Bala Sahitya' Puraskar from Balaanandam Sahitya Vedika.
- 'Telugu Velugu' Puraskar from Telugu Writer's Federation of Chennai.
- 'Ummadi Shetty' Poetry Award for the Poem 'Sanitary Pad'.
- 'Kalimisri' Poetry Award for the Poem 'Madhyalo Ventrukaina Vaddu'.

Other Works:
- So far 20 books have been published. Ten more books are ready for publishing.
- Poems have been published in more than fifty volumes of poetry.

- Some of the poems have been translated into Hindi, English, Kannada, Oriya, Malayalam, and Tamil languages.
- He Translated stories from English, Tamil, Malayalam, and Oriya into Telugu.
- With a travel grant from Kendra Sahitya Akademi, visited the state of Kerala and published a volume of travel poetry called Mattinaipotaanu, from the travel experience.
- Wrote thirty stories, 700 hundred poems, and three novels.

English publications:

1. 'Tiny Treasures' (Collection of Short Stories Translated from Telugu to English) Published by Ukiyoto Publications.
2. 'After a Sleep' poem published in 'Echoes of the Unheard' anthology. Published by 'Thoughts Hymn Publishers.'
3. 'The Unseen Void' English story published in 'Celebrating Together' anthology. Published by Nyra Publishers.
4. 'Broomstick' poem published in 'Verses Unbound (A Tapestry of Voices)' anthology. Published by The Wordings Publications (Delhi).
5. 'A Hand Mill' children's story translated from Telugu to English published in Borderless Journal online monthly magazine.
6. 'Vanaja's Journey to Confidence' children's story translated from Telugu to English published in Kitaab Online Magazine.
7. 'Tangled Hair' Poem published in 'Poetic Worlds Collide Here' anthology. Published by Story Spinners Publications.
8. 'Nocturne' poem published in international-literature-language-journal online magazine.

About the Author

Johny Takkedasila is an Indian Telugu poet, writer, novelist, critic, translator and editor born on 08.06.1991 in Pulivendula, Andhra Pradesh, India. His literary journey, which began as a Telugu poet, has seen the publication of 20 books.

He has received numerous awards for his contributions. The Kendra Sahitya Akademi Yuva Puraskar-2023(National Award) was awarded to "Vivechani," Criticism book in the Telugu language.

His poetry has been featured in many international anthologies, and his stories and poetry have found a place in international magazines. He writes in Telugu, Hindi, and English, demonstrating an ability to translate literature across these three languages.

His literary style appears to aim at making readers contemplate and sensitize society through a compelling narrative. He translated Telugu children's literature stories of different authors into English titled 'Tiny Treasures' which was published by Ukiyoto.

www.ingramcontent.com/pod-product-compliance
Lightning Source LLC
LaVergne TN
LVHW041551070526
838199LV00046B/1909